The Drug Awareness Library

Danger:
TOBACCO

Ruth Chier

The Rosen Publishing Group's
PowerKids Press
New York

Published in 1996 by The Rosen Publishing Group, Inc.
29 East 21st Street, New York, NY 10010

First Edition

Photo credits: Cover by Michael Brandt; p. 16 by Kathleen McClancy; all other photos by Guillermina DeFerrari.

Book Design and Layout: Erin McKenna

Chier, Ruth.
     Danger : tobacco / Ruth Chier.
        p.   cm. — (The Drug awareness library)
     Includes index.
     Summary: Discusses the effects of tobacco on humans and the value
of avoiding its use in any form.
     ISBN 0-8239-2336-3
     1. Cigarette habit—Juvenile literature. 2. Smoking—Juvenile
literature. 3. Tobacco habit—Psychological aspects—Juvenile literature.
4. Nicotine—Physical effect—Juvenile literature.[1. Smoking. 2.Tobacco
habit.] I. Title. II. Series.
HV 5745.C525   1996
362.29'6—dc20   95-50797
                                                  CIP
                                                  AC

613.8
chie e.
c.10
14.95

Manufactured in the United States of America

Contents

What Is Tobacco?   5
Tobacco Is Bad for You   6
Nicotine   9
Tar   10
What Tar Does to the Body   13
What Else Happens?   14
Making Your Life Shorter   17
Tobacco Hurts Everyone   18
Why People Use Tobacco   21
Why Not to Use Tobacco   22
Glossary   23
Index   24

What Is Tobacco?

Tobacco comes from the tobacco plant. Tobacco plants are grown all over the world. Tobacco is used by people all over the world.

The tobacco plant is picked and then dried. The leaves are shredded and made into many different products. Tobacco is usually smoked, as in cigarettes, cigars, and pipes. Sometimes it is chewed, as in chewing tobacco. Many years ago, it was often sniffed through the nose in the form of snuff.

◀ Tobacco comes in many forms.

Tobacco Is Bad for You

It is against the law for people under the age of 18 to buy or use products with tobacco in them. This is because tobacco hurts your body. It contains many **chemicals** (KEM-i-kulz). Several of these chemicals are **toxic** (TOCK-sik). They hurt the body, especially when they are smoked. One of these chemicals is called **nicotine** (NIK-o-teen). Nicotine hurts the body in many ways.

A person must be 18 years or older to buy a tobacco product. ▶

Nicotine

Nicotine is poisonous. It is used to kill insects.

In tobacco, nicotine is **addictive** (a-DIK-tiv). That means that the body **craves** (CRAYVZ) it. A person who smokes cigarettes must keep smoking cigarettes because his body needs the nicotine that is in them.

Nicotine makes a smoker's heart beat too fast. It also makes his hands shaky.

◀ A smoker's body needs to have nicotine in order to feel normal.

9

Tar

Tobacco also contains many other harmful gases and chemicals. When tobacco is smoked or chewed, the gases and chemicals go into the body. They form a brown goop called tar. The tar goes down into the smoker's lungs and stays there. Many smokers have "smoker's cough." This cough is the body's way of trying to get rid of the tar. But it doesn't work.

No matter how someone uses tobacco, tar forms in his lungs. ▶

What Tar Does to the Body

The build-up of tar in a person's lungs makes it hard for a smoker to breathe. A smoker's body can't get all the air it needs. He can't climb stairs or swim or run without feeling tired and out of breath. When he does, his heart has to work very hard to get air. This can make him feel dizzy or sick.

◀ Many smokers have a hard time climbing stairs.

What Else Happens?

Using tobacco, especially smoking it, can cause many problems. Smoking can dull a person's senses of taste and smell. Someone who has smoked for a long time may not be able to smell a turkey baking in the oven or tell what flavor of ice cream he is eating. Smoking can turn a person's teeth and skin yellow. It gives people bad breath and makes their clothes and homes smell of smoke.

Someone who has smoked for a long time has trouble tasting food. ▶

Making Your Life Shorter

Tobacco can cause diseases. Many of these diseases, such as cancer and **emphysema** (em-fi-ZEE-ma), can be **fatal** (FAY-tul).

In fact, each cigarette that a person smokes steals 5 to 20 minutes of that person's life.

◀ Smoking makes a person's life shorter.

17

Tobacco Hurts Everyone

People who smoke tobacco hurt themselves and everyone around them. You may not smoke, but if you stand next to someone who is smoking, you breathe in their smoke. That is called "secondhand smoke." Secondhand smoke can give you a headache or make you tired or dizzy. People who live with smokers risk having many of the same health problems that smokers have.

Breathing in secondhand smoke hurts you almost as much as smoking yourself does. ▶

Why People Use Tobacco

The most common way to use tobacco is by smoking cigarettes. Some people smoke because their friends do. They want to fit in. Some people smoke because they think it makes them seem more grown-up. Other people think smoking will help them relax or lose weight.

None of these things are true. People who smoke are only hurting themselves and the people around them.

◀ Some people smoke because they think it makes them look older.

21

Why *Not* to Use Tobacco

There are many reasons not to use tobacco, especially by smoking.

- Most public places don't allow smoking anymore because it is so bad for people.
- Smoking can get you into trouble at school.
- Smoking hurts you and the people around you.

There are no good reasons to use tobacco.

Glossary

addictive (a-DIK-tiv) Creating a strong, constant
need for a drug.

chemical (KEM-i-kul) The elements that make
something up.

craves (CRAYVZ) Needs something.

emphysema (em-fi-ZEE-ma) A disease of the
lungs often caused by smoking.

fatal (FAY-tul) Something that causes death.

nicotine (NIK-o-teen) Chemical in tobacco.

toxic (TOCK-sik) Something that is poisonous.

Index

B
breath, bad, 14
breathing, 13

C
cancer, 17
chemicals, 6, 10
cigarettes, 5, 9, 17, 21
cigars, 5
craving, 9

G
gases, 10

H
heart, 9

L
law, against smoking, 6

lungs, 10, 13

N
nicotine, 6, 9

P
pipes, 5
poison, 9

S
secondhand smoke, 18
smell, 14
smoking, 5, 6, 9, 10, 14,
    17, 18, 21, 22
snuff, 5

T
tar, 10
taste, 14